First Edition

ISBN 978-1-7322303-1-6

Library of Congress Control Number:  2018913630
Printed in the United States of America

Published by Brown & Lowe Books
Springfield, VA
www.brownlowebooks.com

# Black Bear Goes to Washington

### Written and Illustrated by
### Denise Lawson

*This book is dedicated to the memory of Feisty,*
*a Yukon Quest finisher, who epitomized the spirit of Alaskan sled dogs.*

**Acknowledgements**
Thank you Wayne, Scarlett, Deb, and Greg of Bush Alaska Expeditions for an amazing adventure that went far beyond just learning how to mush.  Thank you Wayne and Scarlett for trusting us to give Black Bear a good retirement home.
Thank you Sacha, Deb, and Ruby for sharing pictures that helped inspire this story.
Thank you Gordon for joining me on the adventures of Black Bear every step of the way, from the dog sled trails of Alaska, to the running trails of Virginia, to the many late nights of book production. I couldn't have done it without you! – D.A.L.

Born in Alaska
knee deep in the snow,
I got all the life lessons
I needed to know.

"Haw" to turn left,
and "gee" to turn right,
teamwork will get you
home before night.

Some call it work,
but for us it is fun.
Lead, wheel, and swing dogs,
we can't wait to run.

We all pull together,
we each pull our weight.
Action is key,
no time for debate.

Our paws may get cold,
our whiskers may freeze,
but at least we don't have
any deer ticks or fleas.

The sun only shines
for part of the day.
To stay warm, we curl up
in a ball on the hay.

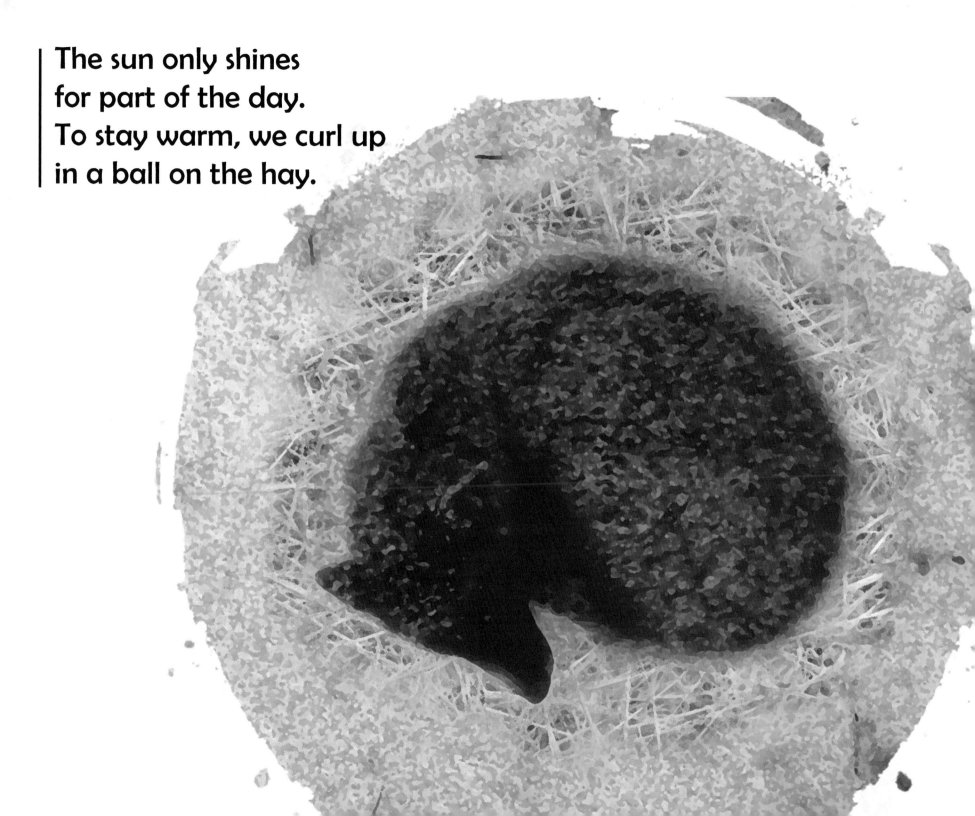

No leashes, no sidewalks, no drama, no fuss.
We just do what we have to, we do what we must.

After 11 cold winters
at 50 below,
it was time to retire.
I was moving too slow.

I arrived from the Yukon
after a very long flight
that took most of a day
and half of a night.

Buildings and monuments
lined every street.
In summer, I discovered
the sweltering heat!

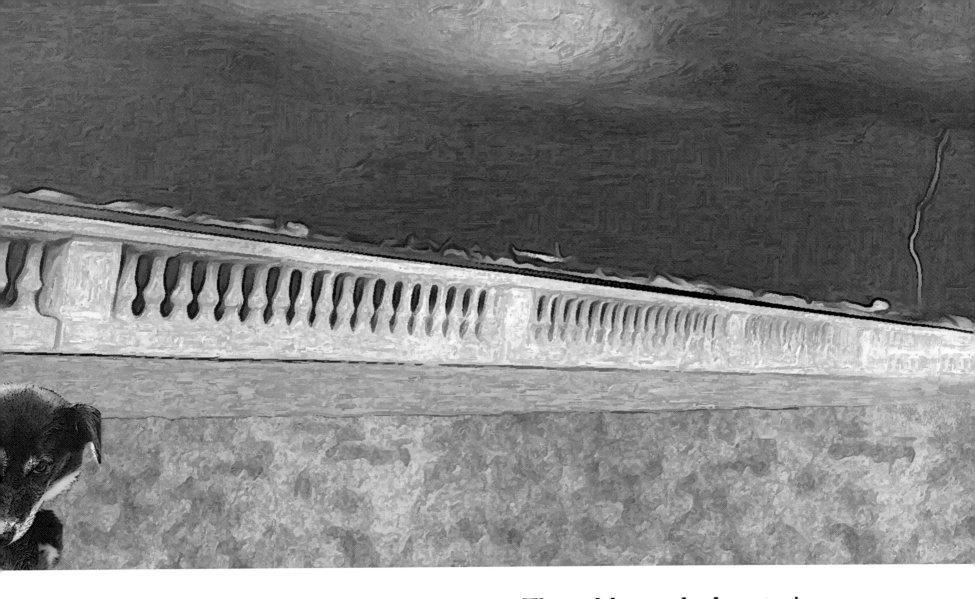

Then I heard about
thunder and lightning.
I found the loud noises
a little bit frightening!

I was told the White House
is a place I must see.
Just one house that's white?
Oh, how can that be?

I thought the White House
would be covered in snow,
like all of the homes
back in Alaska I know.

Bridges that get you
from here to there,
seem to float over water
and cut through the air.

Statues of heroes
and Presidents past,
larger than life and
built to last.

I took a close look
to see...Is he real?
Is he frozen in ice?
Can he move? Can he feel?

This city called Washington
is now my new home.
I hear donkeys and elephants
meet under that dome.

If only they'd let some old
sled dogs come in,
they'd see how to make a
strong team that will win!

To win in Alaska,
means we get there together,
our entire dog team,
through all kinds of weather.

So, come follow me....
my name is Black Bear!

# Black Bear's Guide to Dog Sledding

The musher is the person who drives the sled and gives the commands. Each musher is responsible for the entire dog team. The musher knows the needs and abilities of each dog. Over the years, my mushers always took great care of me. They made sure I had enough food, water, and rest, and they always paid close attention to my feet so I didn't have injuries.

For everyday working, a team doesn't have a set number of dogs. The musher needs to know the weight of the sled and its contents (including the musher) to decide how many dogs are needed on the team. Races, however, have rules about the number of dogs that must start and finish the race. The experience of the musher also determines the number of dogs. The more dogs on the team, the faster the sled will go, so a beginner might start with as few as four dogs.

**Lead dogs** are at the front of the team and set the pace for the rest of the team. They also need to closely follow the musher's commands and help the musher look out for obstacles that the musher might not be able to see. When I was young, I ran as a lead dog in the famous 1,000-mile Yukon Quest sled dog race. I liked being a lead dog because I could see everything in front of me without other dogs blocking my view.

**Swing dogs** are right behind the lead dogs. They help the sled turn around corners. Swing dogs are sometimes lead dogs in training. Before I became a lead dog, I was a swing dog and learned by watching the dogs in front of me. I was lucky to learn from other dogs and mushers who were Yukon Quest veterans.

**Team dogs** run behind the swing dogs. In a large dog team, these dogs would make up most of the team. Dogs don't always stay in the same position. I trust my musher to know when to rotate dogs to different positions.

**Wheel dogs** are the dogs closest to the sled. They are usually the strongest dogs since they have to pull the most weight.

In dog sledding, we have a lot of ropes called lines that look very confusing, but when the team is all connected, the lines help us pull the sled easily. Each dog has a harness which helps us pull the sled comfortably. In the dog yard, we bark excitedly when we see the musher coming to get us with a harness in hand. Pick me! Pick me! I still have my harness even though I am retired. It still smells like Alaska and brings back great memories.

To be a good member of a dog team, you need to be a good listener especially if you are a lead dog. Here are some commands:
**Let's Go** – Start running! This is my favorite command because once that harness is on, I can't wait to run!
**Gee** – Turn right
**Haw** – Turn left
**Easy** – Slow down
**Whoa!** – Stop

# Author's Note

This story was inspired by my real life experience of adopting Black Bear, a retired Alaskan husky sled dog who was a lead dog in the Yukon Quest race in 2009. In January of 2018, I went on a dog sledding expedition several miles outside of Eagle, Alaska. Eagle is a small town along the Yukon River near the US-Canadian border. Very few people live in this part of Alaska. To get there, I flew on a small mail plane from Fairbanks to Eagle and traveled by snow machine (called snow mobile in the "lower 48") to the place where the expedition began. This homestead where Black Bear was born is in the Alaskan bush where there are no roads, no bridges, and no running water. Sled dogs are a necessity to survive. The people here live primarily off of the land. During the short summer months when the river is flowing, they catch thousands of pounds of salmon to provide enough food for themselves and their dogs throughout the harsh winter. Narrow wooded trails and frozen rivers with jumbled ice are the highways of this wilderness. Sometimes the terrain is so rugged that only a dog sled can get through. I had the unique opportunity to learn how to harness and mush my own dog team. Our expedition took us along the Yukon River where the horizon is filled with snow-covered hills and mountains as far as the eye can see. Getting to know the dogs was a very special part of our trip. One of the highlights of this experience was listening to the dogs howling in unison as if to sing a song after their evening meal. Black Bear was one of the most vocal sled dogs on this adventure.

Sled dogs are bred for strength, endurance, temperament and of course, the ability to live in cold temperatures. The puppies get lots of love and interaction before they even start to learn mushing commands. They are handled a lot from birth, so they are comfortable with people putting on their dog harnesses and caring for their feet. Sled dogs develop a remarkable bond with each other and with their handlers. When the dogs are ready to retire from working life, some owners try to find new homes for them where living conditions might be easier. We were very fortunate to be able to adopt Black Bear when she retired in April of 2018.

I wasn't sure how Black Bear would adjust to townhouse living after spending her entire life along the Yukon. She had never seen stairs before and didn't know how to use them. Going up was easier than going down. Everything she encountered was new and different. She quickly adjusted to frequent car rides and eagerly howled to go on any new adventure whether it was a trip to the hardware store or her first 5k race. She approaches life with gusto and enthusiasm and wants to meet everyone who passes by (whether they have two legs or four). We are so happy to have her as a member of our family. She is now fully adjusted to life in the suburbs and enjoys laying in her dog bed by the TV just as much as she loves running on the trails around Washington, DC and Northern Virginia. - D.A.L.

www.blackbearsleddog.com

CPSIA information can be obtained at www.ICGtesting.com
Printed in the USA
LVIW010003230719
624958LV00008BA/26